AF446002

A Purrfect Tale

Skya Papaya

A Purrfect Tale

Skya Papaya

By Sophia Swanson

Dedicated to

Mrs. Feikls, the Creative Writing Club,

Mushu, and Skya Papaya

Contents

1

Moving

My name is Skya, and I am a

Domestic Shorthair, which is a breed of cat.

This is a story about my life, the special

people who are in it, and some challenges

I've gone through.

One sunny day in 2019, I was lying on

my mom and dad's bed, taking a nice nap,

when my Black Cat brother, Midnight, came

into the room.

"Skya, wake up *right now*! I *need* to tell you something!," he yelled at me.

"What do you want?," I asked him, sleepily.

"Haven't you noticed that Mom and Dad have been putting stuff in boxes and talking to the phone a lot lately?"

"Yeah."

"Well, something's wrong. We have to find out what's going on *tonight*! We'd better get working!"

We walked out into the living room where mom was on the couch, crying, and talking to the phone. I jumped up and sat on my mom and Midnight, typical him, sat on the other end of the couch.

"I don't know what to do," she said in a shaky and confused voice, "I really don't know."

Then, the phone said back to her, "Well, think it over. When I had to give one of my cats away, though, I gave away my sweetest because I *knew* he would find his forever home quickly."

"I'll think about it," she said back in a more calm voice than before, "You've helped a lot."

"Bye," the phone said back to her.

"Bye," my mom replied. Then she did what she and Dad call, "Hang up." Then she sighed. "I really don't want to give you away, Skya, but it looks like I have no other choice." Then she petted me and cried some more.

But *what* did she just say? Did she just say she's going to *give me away*? Why would *my own mom* want to give me away? I don't understand humans.

Just then, Dad got home. I rushed to the door to greet him. He seemed sad too. Oh no!

He poured more food and water in our bowls as Mom started cooking Mashed Potatoes and Broccoli for her and Dad.

We all ate dinner and then went to

bed because it was late.

That night, when I was laying in between my

sleeping mom and dad, Midnight came in

and half-whispered, "Skya! We're having a

meeting in the living room *now!*"

I got out of bed and followed him into

the living room, where Luna and Smokey, our

nextdoor neighbors, were sitting. They were

both gray cats, and their fur shone in the

moonlight. The white fur on my chest and

legs seemed to glow. Midnight's black fur

twinkled.

"Tonight's meeting is the most

important meeting of all," Midnight started,

"Today Mom said she was going to *give Skya away*. This is not like her *at all*. We have to find out what's going on."

Just then, the doorbell rang.

"Hide!" said Smokey, but there was nowhere to hide. The couch was gone, the chairs were gone, even the piano was gone. There was only one place left; the litter boxes.

"Where," asked Luna.

"There's only one place left. Come on! Two cats in each box," I said. They were covered litter boxes, so they were the perfect hiding place.

The doorbell rang again. I heard my dad get out of bed and walk down the hallway. He answered the door. "Hello?," he said.

I could see Dad's slippers and another person's boots.

"Hello," another man's voice said, "I work for the moving truck service."

"You're already here?," my dad asked.

"Of course. Right on time.," said the man, "I'm William, by the way."

"I'm Liam. Oh, you were supposed to come at 1:30 *pm* not *am*.," my dad said, puzzled.

"I'm so sorry. I guess Jennifer will be here at 1:30 *pm* then. Bye!" Then William left and Dad went back to bed.

We all stepped out of the litter boxes and sat back down. "Well, I guess we know *something* now. But we still don't know why they're giving Skya away. You two should get home. It's going to be light out soon.," said Midnight.

Luna and Smokey left, and Midnight and I went to bed. I felt sick; I didn't want to leave my home!

That morning, I awoke to the sound of food and water being poured into my dishes. I went running. When I finally reached the water, I drank almost half of it because I had

gotten thirsty over the night. After that, I

used the litter box and went on with a

normal day. Until about an hour later.

My dad brought out the carriers. He

put them both on the floor. He and Mom

chased me around the house and finally

caught me. I wiggled as they put me in a

carrier with a newspaper, a blanket, an open

container of food, and one of those hanging

water bottles that they put in hamster cages.

I panicked. Midnight knew I was leaving for

good and could do nothing about it, so he

came over and we kissed each other for a

long time. We said goodbye and hoped we would see each other again.

After about five minutes, Dad put me in the car and Mom got in, too, but Dad didn't. "Goodbye Skya. Hopefully we'll see each other again soon." Then he closed the rear door of the car.

As we drove away, I knew I was leaving my family, but I knew we would love each other forever.

We rode along, and Mom cracked the windows down just a little, and I could smell that we were quickly moving away from my hometown. After a long time, I finally fell asleep and dreamt of how much I would miss everyone.

When we stopped, I could smell dogs and cats of all different kinds. Mom picked up the carrier that I was in and I could see a building that said on it, "S.P.C.A." Mom brought me into the strange building and stopped at a desk.

"I'm here to drop Skya off," she said.

Oh, now she's going to *drop* me?!

"Okay. If you want to say goodbye to her you can follow me. I'm Olivia," a lady's calming voice answered.

Mom followed her with me and the carrier. When we reached a door, Olivia opened it. There were so many cats! Most of

them were in cages alongside the

walls, but there were a couple cages on the

floor with a few kittens in each. We walked

over to an empty cage and Olivia opened it.

Then she opened my carrier. She pulled me

out and allowed my mom to hold me. I could

tell she was crying, but only a little bit. I

wondered why. I kissed her cheek.

She kissed my nose and said,

"Goodbye, Skya. I love you so much." She was

still crying a little. Then she gave me back to

Olivia and *left*! Why would the mom who had

me since Midnight and I were kittens just

leave me like this? I meowed, but Mom couldn't hear me.

Olivia put me in the new cage and left me there for a few minutes while she talked to someone just outside the room. She had left the door cracked open just a little bit, and I could hear their conversation.

"Hey, what's up?," a man's voice said.

"Well, Riley, we just got a new cat.," Olivia said.

"Where did it come from?," Riley asked.

"From Kane. Her name is Skya. She lived with a woman and a man and another cat that was a little meaner than her.

Her owners had to move to an apartment or

something, but could only keep one cat.

They were lucky the person who owns the

place let them keep the one cat. They gave

Skya away because she was the sweeter one

and they knew she would get adopted faster."

"That's sad. At least she'll get adopted

soon, though."

Olivia came back into the room, but

closed the door the whole way this time. She

took me out of the cage and set me down on

the floor so I could explore.

2

A New Friend

I couldn't see in the cages

beside me, or in the cages below me or in

the cages above me, unless I was out of my

cage. A few days after my mom left me, I was

out of my cage when I looked up. I saw my

cage with my blanket that my mom had

given me when she left. I looked in the cage

to the right of my cage, but there was no cat

in it. I looked in the cage to the left of mine,

and in it was an orange cat with a white

chest, paws, nose and tail tip. He meowed at me, and I meowed back.

"Who are you?," he asked me.

"I'm Skya. Who are *you*?," I said.

"I'm Coral. Hey, you want to be friends with me?"

"Absolutely!"

"You think you can get Olivia to let me out of this cage so we can play together?"

"Oh, yeah," I replied, and walked over to Olivia, who was sitting in the room with the cats. I meowed and headbutted her legs, then ran over to the cage under Coral's, and stood with my two front paws on his cage. I batted the door of it and meowed again.

"Did you make a new friend, Skya?

This is Coral.," she said.

Yeah, I think I know.

She opened the door to Coral's cage

and lifted him out. As soon as his feet

touched the floor, he came running for me.

He sniffed me and I sniffed him. I could tell

we were going to be best friends.

"So what do you want to do first?," he

asked me.

"I don't know," I said, "What do you

want to do?"

"Hmm...," he said with a smile, "I could

teach you how to steal other cat's cat food."

"Sure," I replied.

We went over to a nine-year-old cat's cage where this nine-year-old cat was sleeping. Coral told me his name was Uri.

"Okay, the first thing you need to do is slip your dominant paw through the cage door in a place you can put your paw in the food dish. Then, you dip your paw into the food dish and like a digger truck scoop out some food. Then pull your paw out as quick as you can and eat it right there in front of the cat." While he was instructing, he showed me also. Then he ate the food. "Your turn," he said.

I followed his instructions *exactly*.
Except, when I pulled my paw out I think I
pulled it out too quickly, because all the food
spilled out of my paw. I tried again and when
I pulled my paw out this time, it hit on the
cage door. The metal clanked, and Uri woke
up.

"RAOW!," he screeched.

I quickly darted away before he could
get to me. Coral hissed at him. After that,
Olivia put us back in our cages.

I asked Coral how he got here.

"When I was a kitten, my mom and
brothers and sisters and I were barn cats.
The Farmer didn't know what to do with me

and the other kittens, and there was no

animal shelter for miles, so when we were

about six weeks old, he had to put us in a box

and left us on the side of a road just outside

of a town. Luckily we all survived, thanks to

another stray cat who showed us how to do

a lot of things, including the food stealing

trick I just taught you. She was like another

mom to us. She was completely black, and

her name was Shadow, and we basically *were*

her shadows. We followed her everywhere,

waddling along behind her. One day, Riley

was driving here and he saw all seven of us.

He picked us up one by one and put us in a

large crate in the back of his truck. When we

got here, Rachel checked us for microchips.
Only Shadow had one, but her owners had
died three years before, so she had to stay
here with us. My siblings got adopted, and
finally, Shadow and I were the only two cats
left in our crate. By the time I was a year old,
she got adopted, too. After she left, I was put
in this cage, and I've been in this building for
the past three years, but I have always
known someone will take me home," he told
me.

I was surprised because I thought I
had had a tough time getting here.

"How'd *you* get here?," he asked.

"I lived with two humans and my brother, Midnight. A few days ago, my family had to move, but they could only keep one cat. They chose to give me away because I was the sweeter one and would get adopted faster."

"That's sad, too," said Coral, "Even though I was a stray, I still love humans, but most strays are afraid of them."

"Do you know why you haven't gotten adopted yet?," I asked him.

"I don't know, but it's probably because I was the runt. I think I was too small and fragile for people and apparently people like kittens better than cats so now I guess I'm too old."

I hoped we wouldn't be stuck there forever.

3

Goodbye

Coral and I played a lot. When we

were in our cages, we talked. We hoped we

would be adopted together. But one day our

plans had to change.

A little boy rushed into the room,

saying, "Kika" to every cat in sight. Most of

us tried not to look at him, for he was

extremely annoying, as most two year olds

are. They pull your ears and tail. I don't think

it can get much worse than that. After him

came a woman and a man, and Rachel, one of the shelter workers. I guessed that the man and woman were the boy's mother and father.

The little boy ran over to Coral's cage and pointed at him. "Kika! *Kika!* KIKA," he screamed.

Then his mother said, "Okay, we'll get that kitty cat."

"His name is Coral. Are you going to take the kitty home," asked Rachel.

"Ya, ya, kika kika!"

"Can you say *Coral*," his dad asked.

"Cowill," the boy said slowly.

The mom sat down on the floor and Rachel handed her some papers and a pen and the mom wrote and read for a long time. While she was doing this, Rachel let Coral get out of his cage. I meowed a lot, and Rachel knew I would miss Coral, so she let me out of my cage, too. We played as the boy chased us around a little, or gave us toys or treats. We learned that his name was Oliver.

It finally came to the point where we climbed up on top of the cages because we were so tired from running around.

"Skya, I'm going to miss you," he said, "so I'm giving you my favorite toy that I had found in an alley when I was a kitten." He jumped down to the floor and then into his cage and then onto the floor again and then back up on top of the cages, this time with something yellow in his mouth. He dropped it. It was a yellow cat toy, shaped like a mouse. I picked it up with my teeth.

"Thank you so much Coral. I hope you have a good home," I said to him. My words were muffled because I had the toy in my mouth, but I could tell he could understand me.

When it was time for him to go, we licked noses. We said goodbye. He jumped down and was put into a carrier. I was put back in my cage. As he was leaving with his

new family, I heard him meow, "Goodbye!"

"Goodbye to you too," I meowed back.

I wondered if I would get adopted

soon.

4

Forever Home

After Coral left, I was lonely. I

finally got the hang of stealing Uri's food,

though, and a new cat moved in underneath

me. She had *huge* eyes. It was so funny to

look at her.

Sometimes, people would consider

taking me home with them. One time, an

older boy came in. I'm guessing he was about

fourteen or so.

He took one look at me and said, "Oh, Mom! Look at *this* beautiful feline! I want her so badly! Please can we get her? Please?"

"I'm sorry, John, we can't get a cat! We're just trying to find one for your Aunt Amelia, remember? Besides, your father's allergic to cats. Not today," said his Mother.

Another time, a seventeen year old girl volunteered to help at the shelter. She fell in love with me. Her name was Marie. She wanted to adopt me but couldn't; she said she was lucky her parents let her even volunteer. They were both allergic to all different kinds of animals. I hoped she would be able to get a pet someday, because pets are the best.

One day, a girl who was nine years old walked into the room. Behind her was her mom. The mom asked who was the sweetest cat, and Rachel said, "Skya is the sweetest cat here." She opened my cage and the little girl petted me. She had the biggest smile on her face that I had ever seen!

After a little while, they all left the room and went to a different room with more cats. Rachel put me back in my cage. I could hear that they were playing with some other cats.

Finally, I heard the mom say, "So which cat do you think, Sophia?"

"We should get either Chauncey or Skya." Chauncey was an orange cat in the cat room next door to ours.

"I like those ones, too."

"I think we should get Skya," she said, and I was so happy.

They came back in and told Rachel that they wanted me. She took me out and the girl, whose name was apparently Sophia, played with me and petted me. She also watched me while I stole some of Uri's wet food. He hissed at me. She *could not* stop smiling. She was so happy, and so was I. I could tell that they were taking me to their house.

When they were finally ready, they put me in a carrier along with my blanket and the toy mouse that Coral had given me.

They put the carrier in the back of their car, and Sophia climbed in the back with me. Even though the windows weren't down, I could smell that this car had been all over my town.

I meowed the whole way there because maybe I could see Mom, Dad and Midnight again! It finally got to the point where the scent of my town was so strong that it was the only thing I could smell. While

I was meowing, Sophia was telling me

that it is okay.

My newest mom opened the back of

the car and took out a litter box and a bag of

toys and asked Sophia, my new sister, if she

would stay in the car with me and she said

she would. We stayed in the car for a few

minutes, and I meowed some more. Sophia

tried to pet me through the door of the cage,

but it didn't work so well. Her hands would

not fit enough to pet me, but if I got close

enough to the cage door, she could sort of

pet me. She said that I was the fluffiest cat

she had ever touched.

When her Mom came back, she took more stuff into their house, and I decided I'd call her Mom because it seemed like I'd be living with them. When Mom came back, she took out the carrier and Sophia got out, too.

Then, we walked along a sidewalk for about two seconds. I was *sure* that I was in the town that my mom and dad and Midnight lived in. I was so excited! Mom carried me up about 20 stairs and into an apartment. There was a little girl about four years old, a little boy about one year old, and their great aunt. Mom brought me into the living room and the kids surrounded the cage I was in. Mom told them to back up and then Sophia opened my cage. I sniffed around and finally decided to come out. Then Mom picked me up and brought me to a corner with a litter box and a food and water dish.

I did not like to be picked up and I did not like the noise that the little kids were making. As soon as she put me in the litter box, I ran to the nearest thing I could hide under and laid down. I was under a long, blue couch with metal things probably used to recline.

Sophia's sister, Chelsea, and their brother, Brian, got on top of the part of the couch that I was under, and Sophia was laying on the floor behind the couch, watching me and trying to get me to come out. When she saw that her siblings' weight made the underside of the couch go down and almost squished me, she yelled, "Get off the couch! You're squishing Mu- I mean Skya!" They immediately jumped off the couch and the couch no longer was about to squish me.

Then they got out the cat laser and shined it under the couch for me, and I chased it, but only under the couch. I did not want to come out yet because I knew I would basically be attacked by Chelsea and Brian.

Finally, after a little while they left me alone and I took a nice long nap. Sophia came to check on me once in a while, but I didn't really mind because she was patient and knew that everything was new to me. In fact, within the first half hour, I had already considered her my sister.

After a few hours, Chelsea, Brian and Sophia went to bed. I came out and explored. I learned where everything was and ate some cat food. I also found out that if I dipped my food in my water it would taste like Uri's wet food. It was so delicious!

Finally I walked out to the doorway of the bathroom where Mom was standing and started bathing myself. She told Sophia I was

out from under the couch and that she could

come play with me for a few minutes.

She got out of bed and started petting

me. After a while, I walked out to the living

room and laid down next to the couch. She

got out a little thing that looked like a mouse

and pointed it to the floor. Then she pressed

the nose and a little red light appeared on

the floor. I knew it was a cat laser, so I

chased it. I had to catch it someday soon! I've

heard that if a cat catches the laser, that cat

will become the most famous cat in the

world, and have even more money than kings

and queens, and I would buy all the treats

and open a treat store with laser disco parties. Sophia made the laser go all over the place, and I couldn't catch it. I finally just gave up and decided to try again the next day.

After a while, Sophia went to bed and fell asleep while I figured out I could sleep on the back of the couch. That's where I slept that night. I was so happy that I had found a home.

The next morning, I woke up to blackness outside the window. I was used to getting up early in the morning. But normally the humans were up by now. I started meowing and meowing. Finally, Sophia got up with me. I could tell she was still very tired but I just wanted to be with her. She said that it was only 5:00 in the morning and that she would only get up with me this early this one time. Then she laid down on the couch and fell back to sleep, so I took a nap on the back of the couch.

5

Alone

Sophia took care of me, fed me,

petted me, and cuddled me, and Chelsea was

alright, but Brian was terrible! He was only

about one year old, but I still didn't like him.

He slobbered and cried all the time and he

made a mess when he ate. I decided he was

not my friend. He was worse than a dog!

The entire family stayed home with

me for the next day, and then they all left the

day after that. Sophia had said that she had

to go to school, Mom had to go to work, and Chelsea and Brian had to go to the babysitter's, TT's house. I was sad that I had no one to snuggle with but was glad that I got the day away from Brian. That day, since I hadn't known what was going on yet, I ran around the house meowing. I wanted someone to play with and to cuddle with while my family was gone.

Finally, they came back home! I was so happy- except for Brian coming home.

Later that night, Sophia told me that she had had another cat before me. Her name was Mushu Dondonce Swanson and she had died the year before. She also said that they loved each other so much that

Mushu would climb up in her bunk bed and

they would go into her sleeping bag and they

would fall asleep together. I wish humans

could understand cats because if they could,

I would tell her that I feel sorry that her cat

died, and that I love her so much.

The same thing happened the next

day. The humans left, I cried and was lonely,

but after a while I didn't really care if they

left. As long as it wasn't for a long time.

Mostly every day went the same, until

one of the best things in my life happened.

6

Dad

After a couple of weeks at my new

home, someone came to the door in the

afternoon. I ran to the door to greet whoever

it was. Chelsea and Sophia ran to the door

screaming, "Daddy!" Brian just sat where he

was, blowing bubbles out of his disgusting

little mouth. The lock unlocked from the

outside, and the apartment door opened.

There stood a man in the doorway, and

according to Sophia and Chelsea, he was

their dad. He had two big bags in his hands.
He came through the door, set down his
bags, and Chelsea and Sophia gave him a
hug.

"We got a kitty, Daddy," Chelsea said.

I could tell Dad was not impressed
with me, because he just stared at me. I
would try to be his friend, even though he
seemed like an enemy.

He went into his bedroom, laid down,
and fell asleep. I jumped up with him and he
didn't pet me, so I meowed in his ear. He
pushed me away, so I decided I was done. I
jumped off the bed and thought, "I'll just

have to try again later." I walked out to the living room where I could get attention.

The next day when Dad came out, he sat down on the couch and started watching TV, which is a very stupid thing for humans to do when they could be outside or better yet, be paying attention to their cat. I jumped up with him and rubbed on him, but he completely ignored me. After a while, he shooed me off the couch. Then Sophia picked up the cat laser and pointed it on the floor near me, and I chased it, until it went over a blanket. I laid down on the blanket and waited for the dot to not be paying attention-- then I would pounce. I waited a while and then Sophia got bored, so she put

the cat laser away.

On nights when Sophia didn't have to

go to school the next day, the kids watched a

movie, which they called, "Movie Night." On

other nights, they went to bed.

Dad continued to either ignore me or

push me away, until one day when Sophia

said, "Be nice to her!" A couple of days later,

just before I was about to give up, I hopped

up beside Dad, and he started petting me! I

was so happy that he had finally realized

what he was supposed to do! It might've

been the best day of his life!

7

Summer

a few months later, one day, Sophia

came home from school and set down her

bookbag and didn't do any homework. I

wondered what was going on because I had

never lived with kids before this.

I followed her into her room where

she unplugged the alarm clock and took it

out to the room with the washer and dryer,

the room they called, "outback." They called

it that because it was in the back of their house.

The next day, Sophia was supposed to go to school, but she didn't. This happened occasionally either because she was sick or it was a holiday. Being sick was not good, but I could tell that it must have been a holiday, because everyone was as happy as could be, except for Mom, who still had to go to work. I was happy that I had someone to play and cuddle with.

I also noticed that it was much hotter out and that the sun was up earlier and down later. Dad had also brought out the air conditioner earlier that month.

Sophia stayed home the next day, too. Once she stayed home for about a week for a holiday called Easter. Maybe we were having Easter *again*? Then she didn't go to school for an entire week! She told Dad it was Summer and she wanted to go swimming, but he just laid on the couch and watched YouTube. Finally, he took Chelsea, Sophia, and Brian outside for a few hours. When they came back, they were damp and smelled like chlorine. They got baths, had dinner and watched TV.

About a month passed and then my family started packing, and Mom said Leah would watch me. Leah was Mom's best friend. She had three dogs, which is three too many dogs! I did not want *her* looking after me!

The next day, my family left me! Sophia hugged me, kissed me, and said goodbye. The day after they left, Leah came over.

8

Not So Bad

When Leah first came in the door,

I ran to it because I thought it was my family.

When she opened the door, though, I ran

into the bedroom to hide. I heard her get a

bag out from under the sink and scoop the

litter box. She put food in my food dish and

water in my water dish. Then she turned on

Dad's scanner so I didn't feel as lonely. Dad

was a firefighter, so he had a scanner. Leah

sat on the couch after that and visited for a

while. I poked my head around the corner to see what she was doing.

The next day, Leah came again. I sat in the middle of the living room floor and stared at her. Here's a little secret: she's weird. She has *dogs* and that's why. Well, It's not really a secret, is it? She gave me more food and water and scooped my litter box. Then she walked over to me and tried to pet me! I sniffed her and then almost instantly ran away. She smelled like disgusting dogs! I ran and hid under the bed. Leah stayed around for about twenty minutes, then she had to leave. I was so relieved that she had to leave.

She came the next day too. I also found out she had horses, which aren't as bad as dogs, but still, I'd rather not go near those big, scary, smelly beasts. I was thankful she gave me more food and water and scooped my litter box, but she was still so annoying. That day, she took a picture of me and sent it to Mom. Apparently Mom replied, "Aww, cute! The girls are so excited to see her when we come back," because Leah said that she had said that. I couldn't wait to see them either, and I couldn't wait for Leah to leave and not come back. Finally after about an hour of being annoyed by Leah, she left to feed her horses.

Around 2:00 a.m. I started thinking about Leah. I was lucky to have her to feed me and give me water. Without her, I might've starved with my family out of town. I had just realized how lucky I was to have Leah look after me. Even though I didn't like dogs and their smell that was all over her, she didn't bring her dogs or horses up here, so that was okay. But I still decided to stay away from her for the next couple of days just to make sure she was okay.

The next day, I spied on her from under the couch while she refilled my water dish, and it seemed like she was okay. I ran over to the water dish and took a little sip

out of it to show Leah that I appreciated it.
Then she filled my food dish and scooped my
litter box. When I was sure she was all right
to go near, I rubbed on her legs. That is a
cat's way of saying, "thank you," or, "I love
you." This one was a "thank you." She bent
down to pet me, but I ran away. I wasn't one
hundred percent sure she was okay yet.

It was Thursday. Hopefully my family
would be back any day now. But that day I
discovered something amazing about Leah.

I smelled it on her for the first time. It
was other cats! This was amazing! It was a
miracle! I instantly rubbed up against her
and started licking her. She sat down on the

couch and I laid down beside her. She stroked my silky fur for almost twenty minutes, and the whole time I was purring. Leah said it sounded like a motorcycle was outside because my purrs of delight were so loud.

I had one more day with Leah. She was one of my best friends now. The last day she did her usual routine with my food and water and litter box. Then we snuggled and she petted me and I purred. Then she played with me. I had so much fun! We played with the cat laser, which I can never seem to catch. We played with the yellow mouse Coral had given me at the animal shelter. We played with the elephant toy that squeaked whenever it moved even just the tiniest bit. Leah and I played with a lot of toys for about half an hour.

When Leah left, I was glad she had taken care of me, but sad she had to leave.

The next day, my family came home. They all said I looked smaller, and I knew why. They said they had gone to their grandma's and grandpa's house for the week, and they had a much taller, meaner cat than me.

Sophia asked me, "Were you good for Leah?"

I replied with a meow.

A couple days later, Sophia ran into the living room. She said, "I just came up with the *perfect* nickname for Skya! How about Skya Papaya!?"

I decided it *was* the perfect nickname, and my family still calls me Skya Papaya.

I was just as glad to make a new friend that week as I was for my family to be back.

Pictures of Skya Papaya

SKYA

Author's Note

I have always wanted to write a book about my cat, Skya Papaya, but I never had the time or patience to do it, and even if I did, I would've forgotten about it in about a week. I joined Creative Writing club so I could write books and publish them.

Most of the things in this book actually happened to my cat, like having to move away from her first family the way she did in the book, living in the S.P.C.A., and obviously being adopted again. Other things, like meeting Coral the cat at the S.P.C.A. and most of the people at the beginning of the

book, were probably not true.

Hopefully next year I decide to write a

longer book about Skya and her adventures

or maybe a series. I really hope you liked

reading this book and seeing a cat's view of

the world.

About the Author

Sophia Swanson is a middle school student who loves reading and animals, especially cats and dogs. She lives in an apartment in Pennsylvania with her Mom, Dad, brother, sister, and her cat, Skya Papaya. She also likes to draw, play basketball, and helped organize a bake sale to raise money for two animal shelters.

A little cat going through big changes

Skya Papaya is a small pet domestic shorthair cat who has the perfect life until she has to move away from her family. She loves her family, but there is no way she can stop her humans from moving to an apartment which will only allow the family to keep one cat.

She goes to an animal shelter where she makes a new friend and is adopted by another loving family. She learns to live with them and goes on funny and crazy adventures around the house and makes a most unexpected best friend who owns three dogs.